Tales of the
Old North Woods

A Collection of Wildlife Adventures

Roy W. Harper

Tales of the Old North Woods / A Collection of Wildlife Adventures

This is a work of fiction.
Author's email: talesoftheoldnorthwoods@gmail.com
Page on Facebook: Tales of the Old North Woods

Scripture quotations are taken from the *Holy Bible*, New Living Translation, copyright © 1996. Used by permission of Tyndale House Publishers, Inc., Wheaton, Illinois 60189. All rights reserved.

Cover Design created in CreateSpace by the author and his wife

Photographs in this book were taken by the author with the exception of the following pictures:
page 11 Northern Water Snake-Wesley Douglas Lapointe-shutterstock.com
page 13 Snapping Turtle-Ethan Daniels-shutterstock.com
page 26 Beaver-Annette Shaff-shutterstock.com
page 27 Woodland Caribou-Howard Sandler-shutterstock.com
page 34 Black Bear-Mircea Costina-shutterstock.com
page 37 Brown Bat-Geoffrey Kuchera-shutterflock.com
page 97 Rainbow Trout-pu_kibun-stutterstock.com
page 66 Red-Winged Blackbird-Birdegal-shutterstock.com
page 67 River Otter-Magdanatka-shutterstock.com
page 72 Moose-Jim Cumming-shutterstock.com
page 75 Gray Wolves-Martin Mecnarowski-shutterstock.com
page 78 Opossum-Kathy Clark-shutterstock.com
page 91 Blue Jay-FotoRequest-shutterstock.com
page 95 Bobcat-andamanec-shutterstock.com
page 105 Barred Owl-Manuel Lacoste-shutterstock.com
page 124 Water Scene-Vern Poll
Back Cover Author Photograph-Rebecca Hamilton Facebook: Rebecca's Photography

Editor: Leta Luurtsema
Email: leta.editing@gmail.com

ISBN-13: 978-1542683807
ISBN-10:1542683807

Library of Congress Control Number: 2018904480

Printed by CreateSpace Independent Publishing Platform, North Charleston, South Carolina, United States of America

Dedication

To my children and grandchildren, with love and hope.
It was because of your tender hearts, eager listening ears, and
affirming smiles, that these tales were told.

Acknowledgements

My utmost gratitude goes to my dear wife, Dawna, who never once questioned my calling to write this book. Even when the words would not come, she'd bring a smile and a kiss to keep the dream alive. In addition, no one but God will ever know how many times she saved this book from my lack of skills on the computer.

I must also mention my four children, who helped and encouraged me in so many ways. This was a wonderful family effort. Thank you Bethany, Rebecca, Cassie and Justice.

Other family members and friends who gave of their time and efforts for the cause were Becky Gerhart, Karen Hamilton, Marcie Poll, Vern Poll, Payton Saunders, Jordan Racey and Dr. James Carlson. Thank you for caring and sharing your wisdom.

Special thanks and recognition go to my editor, Leta Luurtsema. She patiently made sense of my ramblings, and made me look more like a writer than I ever thought possible. This slow learner has learned much from her, but I shall forever need her for my commas!

Final acknowledgement goes to my parents, Charlene and Jack, who led a mischievous son to pursue grand adventures in the outdoors. I would have never found *The Old North Woods,* or, more importantly *The Great Creator,* without them.

Table of Contents

Introduction

"Tales of the Old North Woods" is a collection of fictitious short stories that take place in a magnificent wilderness area long ago. My family's imagination first found this place near bedsides and campfires when our children were quite young. Somehow, my spirit for storytelling helped their favorite animals come alive. Adventures were born while night-light beams or flickering flames set aglow their grinning, marshmallow-smeared faces.

Together, we explored a place where no one had ever set foot, and animals possessed the ability to talk and reason as we do. Much like us, these creatures made both good and bad decisions, with both used by the Great Creator to teach important truths and lessons. Passing on these discoveries, and giving their divine source His proper honor and glory have always been my foremost goal. Explaining things such as why loons sing and beavers have flattened tails, admittedly, has added a dash of truth-stretching fun to these stories. I have never been able to stop myself from such shenanigans, nor can I bring myself to apologize for it!

These days, my children are starting to have their own children, and passing on the family tradition of "Tales of the Old North Woods" seems to be the natural thing for this Grandpa to do. Perhaps this is my legacy. If so, it is my hope and prayer that by putting these words in writing, this legacy might even reach beyond my family into yours. If only one soul should fall in love with their Great Creator because of the simple words written in this book, I will know that I have left behind something very worthwhile.

So grab some marshmallows, and fill your head with the vision of a quiet lake that's surrounded by tall pines and rocky shores... where spirits are lifted by the Prayer Bird call.

Ask the animals, and they will teach you.
Ask the birds of the sky, and they will tell you.
Speak to the earth, and it will instruct you.
Let the fish of the sea speak to you.
They all know that the LORD has done this.
For the life of every living thing is in his hand...
Job 12:7-10

Chapter 1

The Prayer Bird Call

Way back in a time that only the ancient trees remember, a beautiful loon spent her summers fishing a cool, clear lake in the heart of the Old North Woods. She loved the water and the sky, but she was terribly clumsy on land. For this reason, she avoided the shoreline and the animals who lived there. She would even dive under the water and swim away if anyone came near. She was a very shy bird indeed.

After a while, the other animals began to think poorly of her. They mistakenly thought that she was a proud bird who felt she was better than them. "Look at her," they would scoff. "Not one elegant black or white feather out of place. She's far too lovely to be seen with the likes of us!" Of course, she didn't feel that way at all, and she hated being so misunderstood. Not knowing what else to do about the situation, the broken-hearted loon spent her days alone, out near the middle of the lake.

Then, it happened: One day, two of the lake's most notorious villains noticed her. A wickedly long water snake and a frightfully huge snapping turtle conspired together to hatch an evil plot against the vulnerable and unprotected bird. Neither of them liked sharing the lake's fish with the loon, and both were jealous of her noble elegance. The snake was sly, but a coward. From his mouth came venomous words of hate. The ill-tempered old turtle was the self-proclaimed "Lord of the Lake," and everyone feared him. Staying in his good favor meant agreeing with his title, and often those with a different opinion disappeared if they got too close to the lake's edge! The two decided that it would be the snake's job to distract the loon, while the turtle rose up from beneath the water's surface to snatch her, and drag her under. It was a dreadful plan for sure!

The next morning, a thick cloud of fog formed, and slowly made its way across the still waters. Seizing this opportunity, the water snake emerged from some cattails and swam out to sneak along within it. By the time the misty gray veil passed over the unsuspecting loon, the snake was nearly upon her. She was startled when he whispered, "Greetings, despised and exiled one!" His sudden presence and the harshness of his words were magnified because she couldn't see him. She thought to escape, but which way should she flee? His hushed accusations came again, this time from a different hidden location.

"You must have done something very terrible to be banished way out here all alone, in such a dreary place. I'm thinking that no one would even come to your rescue if you were to cry out for help. What a helpless feeling that must be!" Sensing her confused panic, the snake continued to circle her, all the while hissing more quiet lies.

Meanwhile, way down in the deep, dark depths of the lake, a pair of beady turtle eyes and a sinister

turtle smile popped up through the silt. The eyes watched as a pair of webbed feet kicked and dangled enticingly above them. 'This is going to be easy,' he thought, as he pushed up from the muck and began his assent. But in doing so, a large gas bubble was released from the decaying matter beneath him. It rolled out from beneath his great shell and raced ahead of him to the surface. The nasty smell and the sound of the bubble bursting on the surface were more than enough to warn the loon that trouble was coming from beneath her, as well!

'I am doomed!' she thought. So she did the only thing she could do... she cried out to the One who holds the life of every living thing in His hand... the Great Creator! Such a cry of distress had never before been heard in the Old North Woods. Her haunting, mournful wail carried far beyond the wilds that surrounded the lake, even beyond the distant hills and mountains. As it traveled, it pierced deeply into the hearts of all the creatures that heard it. Each stopped what they were doing and remained very still, listening in silent reverence, as if a queen were speaking.

But hatred can be very strong, and the water snake tried to silence her by striking one last time at her failing spirit: "The Creator will not save you! Can you not see that His fearful cloud of judgment is upon you?" Likewise, the snapping turtle was gaining momentum as he clawed his way upward and closer. His long, wrinkly neck was extended and his bony beak was wide open as he focused on the leg he was about to crush. His anger overwhelmed him as he thought of her being a "Queen" on his lake! 'I will silence her singing now!'

No one in all the Old North Woods could have expected what happened next…

"ENOUGH!"

The single word came like an explosion. Its shock wave instantly destroyed the foggy shroud that had imprisoned the lake.

The Great Creator had spoken, and the cowardly snake was completely exposed! And with that one word, the brilliant sun cut down through the gloomy darkness and blinded the turtle! Now, both the accuser and the executioner were harmless, and each fled in a frantic search for a shadow… but none were to be found! Such is the power of one word from the Great Creator, maker of light and all things good!

The animals of the Old North Woods began to gather on the shores all around the golden lake. The loon couldn't imagine why, until a raccoon called out: "Could you ask the Great Creator to forgive me for my stealing?" And a doe deer cried: "Can you ask the Great Creator to give me a fawn?" On and on it went, each of them asking her to speak to the Great Creator on their behalf. All who knew Him, sensed His love in her, and with each prayer she prayed with them, she could feel the fire of His Spirit growing inside her. Before the day was over, everyone would come to know her as the 'Prayer Bird.'

To this very day, the call of the loon is symbolic of wilderness places. It is most often heard in the early morning and at the end of the day, the times when we most often share heartfelt matters with the Great Creator. So, if you are ever blessed enough to hear a loon, please take notice as it sings, that a hush still falls over the Old North Woods, just as it should when someone is praying!

The Lord is far from the wicked,
but he hears the prayers of the righteous.
Proverbs 15:29

17

Chapter 2

The Mask and Rings

A raccoon's perspective of "The Prayer Bird Call"

Way back in a time that only the ancient trees remember, a good-hearted raccoon lived in a crooked maple tree, deep in the Old North Woods. He spent his nights catching delicious crayfish that hid in the shallow weeds and rocks of a cool, clear lake that was just down the hill. When morning came he would return to his favorite tree to snooze away the day. It was a pretty good life for the little fella, except for one problem: he had no family. This was because he had made a promise to the Great Creator to try to live his life honestly. Of course, this had terrible consequences for the converted crook, because from the day raccoons are born, stealing is their way of life.

His parents had told him the black mask on his face and black rings around his tail were undeniable proof that he had been created to steal. He had to admit, that on more than a few occasions he had stolen things and enjoyed it, much like any other raccoon would. Sensing that he would never be able to convince his family otherwise, and that it would be too hard for him to keep his promise if he stayed, he left them to search for the truth about his mask and rings.

As the days went by, the curious raccoon stayed awake longer and longer, watching the world beneath his bent tree. From his hiding place, he could study the comings and goings of the other woodland creatures without their knowledge. Each day a new chapter in the Old North Woods unfolded beneath him, and he found pleasure in the viewing. Chipmunks teased and chased each other. Small flocks of black-capped chickadees chirped and chattered

as they fluttered about, pecking for insect morsels on leaves and limbs. He saw fights fought, love won and lost, babes born, and last breaths breathed. He took it all in, stealing each moment without consent and hiding them in his heart. Sometimes he wondered if he was still a thief after all.

One particular daily visitor had found a soft spot in his heart. She was a sleek, reddish-brown whitetail deer that was always alone. She followed a little-used trail through a patch of tall ferns that led down to the lake. There, the doe would drink and bed down for the day. He saw great sorrow in her eyes, and he wanted to comfort her. But how could he, without revealing the fact that he had been spying on her? Her soft, lonely crying during the spring birthing season was almost more than he could endure. Like the doe, he also longed to have a family.

In the world of nature, things are always changing. Winds change direction, and sometimes die down to nothing at all. Large waves turn into small ripples, and then go calm. Violent storms turn into sunshine and rainbows. Sometimes these events can change a life.

On one unusual morning, the air suddenly turned cool and damp just as the doe entered the ferns. The raccoon watched her timidly pause, with tail twitching and ears erect, assessing the situation. Her body stiffened as a monstrous wall of fog slowly climbed up the hill from the lake to meet her. Sensing danger, and seeing that her path to the lake's edge was now blocked, she resigned herself to lying down in the ferns. The raccoon lost sight of her and everything else as the fog covered the whole woods. He felt scared and uneasy with his inability to see, and he worried about the doe. So he prayed to the Great Creator, begging for protection for her, and himself.

When a long, haunting cry came from the lake, the startled raccoon nearly fell out of his tree. The mournful wail deeply pierced his heart. The call had found the heart of the doe as well, for she could be heard answering with her own soft bleats. She wanted desperately to go towards the sad sound. It seemed that even while it was a distressing song, she still found hope in it. The raccoon could hear her getting up and tripping in the ferns. Then he could hear her thrashing and crashing blindly in the trees. Her soft cries were turning into loud, uncontrolled bawling.

Before he could even think of it, he heard his mouth say, "Hold still. I will come and help you!" Before he could even think that she would not want help from a spying thief, or that it might not be possible to find her in such a thick fog, he had already felt his way down the tree and all the way over to her side. He calmly reassured her as he gently stroked her front leg, "Don't be afraid, my hands are my eyes, and I will get you where you need to go."

Only someone who had spent his whole life catching and stealing food from places where his eyes could not look would dare to do what that little raccoon was doing. It was with those skills that he led her each step of the way, slowly following the voice from the lake and guiding her around all obstacles. Upon reaching the water's edge, they stopped to consider if they should proceed…

No one, in all of the Old North Woods, expected what happened next. Another voice, one of undisputed power and authority, shook the earth,

"ENOUGH!"

The blast of the Great Creator's voice instantly cleared the fog and unveiled an elegant, sun-glistening loon in the center of the lake. Even from a distance, her eyes seemed ablaze with a fire that burned from somewhere deep within her. She was like no other bird they had ever seen or heard, and it seemed as if the Great Creator was appointing her to some high honor.

Realizing this, all the other animals began to gather on the shores around the golden lake. Caught up in the moment, and realizing that the loon had been given the Spirit of love and prayer, the excited little raccoon could not help himself, and he called out, "Could you ask the Great Creator to forgive me for my stealing?" Then, the equally excited doe cried out, "Can you ask the Great Creator to give me a fawn?" Others joined in with their requests, and she was more than happy to guide them all into the prayerful presence of the Great Creator. Soon, they all began to refer to her as the 'Prayer Bird.'

After they had all prayed, the doe turned, and for the first time, took a good long look at the little fellow who had bravely brought her down to the water. The raccoon grew nervous and asked her, "Do you mind the company of a thief?" The doe's reply came as the long awaited answer in his search for truth, "I could not see you as a thief in the fog, nor do I see you as a thief now. Did you not see the glorious, full black mask that the Prayer Bird wore on her head? Did you not see the noble black ring around her neck? If masks and rings are the marks of a thief, then she is a grander one than you!" With that, they both laughed much harder than they had laughed in a long, long time.

The two went on to become the best of friends. They would even call themselves 'family'…which, not surprisingly, grew the next spring, when the raccoon became an 'uncle,' with the arrival of two finely spotted fawns!

Each time he said,
"My gracious favor is all you need.
My power works best in your weakness."
So now I am glad to boast about my weaknesses,
so that the power of Christ may work through me.
II Corinthians 12:9

Chapter 3

The Hero of Beaver Tail Lake

Way back in a time that only the ancient trees remember, there was a magnificent lake in the Old North Woods. Its shores teemed with plants and animals and its depths swarmed with many kinds of fishes. Spring rains and melting snow always kept the lake filled with cool, clear water. Often, animals would travel great distances from surrounding areas just to be refreshed at this wonderful place.

Soon, word of this famous lake reached the twitching ears of a great herd of wandering caribou, and the entire herd began the long and dangerous journey to the lake. Only the Great Creator Himself could count their numbers, and almost everything in their path along the way was either eaten or trampled into the ground.

After many days of travel, the terribly thirsty caribou entered a deep valley that would lead them to the lake. The valley was so narrow and rugged that the caribou were forced to stay on the trail. With the passing of each caribou's sharp trotting hooves, the trail to the lake was dug deeper and deeper. Even the lake's bank was worn away as the excited caribou jumped into the water to drink and bathe.

Suddenly a deep rumbling was felt throughout the entire Old North Woods. Then…CABOOSH! The water burst out of the lake and flowed down the path that the caribou had made! About half the caribou herd was washed away by this newly formed river, and to this day the two herds have never gotten back together. The herd that was washed away stayed in the soggy barren grounds and the other herd still lives up in the woodlands.

As the days passed, the river kept flowing and the lake got smaller and smaller. The water was turning into dried-up mud. The fish were running out of room to swim and the plants were starting to die. Many of the animals who lived around the lake were beginning to leave, and the long, sad call of the Prayer Bird echoed through the Old North Woods.

Ah, but all was not lost! There were stirrings within a large mound of sticks and mud that lay on the edge of a distant pond. A web-footed creature, with rich brown fur, emerged from within, and stood about a deer's-leg tall on her lodge. She cupped her ears for better hearing, and recognized the distressed calls of her loon friend. She stamped upon her roof three times, and almost before she finished the third- three small beaver heads appeared in the water beneath her. She used no words, for each young one knew that when "Momsie" stamped her foot, there was work to do!

A day of cross-country travel later, Momsie and her trio arrived at the shrinking lake. Seeing the urgency of the situation, they wasted no time getting to work. They quickly began chewing through the trunks of shoreline trees with their large, sharp teeth. Soon, tall birch, aspen, maples and  willows were falling in every direction. Cutting down trees was very dangerous work, but the wood was essential for making a wall that would stop the water leaving the lake. The logs and brush were dragged to the water, and then floated across the lake to the construction site.

For a little while everything was going well, but as we all know, sometimes when we try to get things done too quickly, accidents happen. As the story goes, it seems one well-meaning beaver was in such a hurry to get a tree to fall over that he failed to notice his sibling working in the same area. With one last big bite, the huge tree creaked and cracked and then fell upon the poor animal with a terrible crash! Realizing what had happened and fearing the worst, the other beavers rushed over to see if they could do anything to help their unfortunate family member.

Much to their amazement, when they found him, he was alive! Not only that, he was squealing like the dickens and pulling on his tail as hard as he could, trying to get it out from under the tree! It took all the beavers putting their shoulders to the tree to get it lifted off his tail, and as it came out from under the tree, they were shocked! For you see, up until this day, all beavers had thick, round, furry tails- much like that of a river otter. Now they were looking at a hairless tail that was flatter than a skipping stone, and it sure looked like it hurt!

No one knew what to say to the little guy as he stared at his oddly injured tail through small beaver tears. Yet, before anyone could even think of anything to say… even to say they were sorry… something amazing happened. Without blaming anybody, or making any fuss whatsoever, the beaver simply turned and dragged his flattened tail over to the tree that had fallen on it, and went back to work! Seeing that nothing could keep this faithful worker from completing the task that was before him, the rest proudly joined in as well.

Of course, the Great Creator had been watching all this and He was greatly pleased. He blessed the beavers' efforts, and in a short time the huge strong wall, which we call a dam, was finished. Very little water leaked through this dam, and because the Great Creator sent rain, the lake was saved. Soon, the lake's shores once again teemed with plants and animals, and its depths swarmed with many kinds of fishes. To honor their hero, everyone began referring to these cool, clear waters as "Beaver Tail Lake."

Since that time, the Great Creator has made the beaver His special caretaker of all the lakes and ponds in the Old North Woods, and all beavers have been born with flat tails to remind us of this story. These days, should any of us ever forget to apply this lesson of hard work and dedication to our own lives, our friend the beaver will be more than happy to remind us… by spanking its flat tail on the surface of the beautiful calm waters of the Old North Woods.

The master was full of praise.
'Well done, my good and faithful servant.
You have been faithful in handling this small amount,
so now I will give you many more responsibilities.
Let's celebrate together!'
Matthew 25:21

Chapter 4

Big Bear's Rainbow

Way back in a time that only the ancient trees remember, a proud Mama Bear gave birth to a single bear cub in the Old North Woods. The cub grew fast on his mama's milk, and loved to explore the area around his den, looking for things to chew on, dig up or sniff. He was very happy.

Then one day, after a hard summer's rain, Mama Bear took her cub down to the meadow near Beaver Tail Lake. She had a big surprise for him! As they entered the clearing, the cub noticed that the entire meadow was full of animals that had come from all around the Old North Woods. They all seemed to be staring up into the sky. Mama Bear motioned for her cub to look up as well. He stood on his stubby hind legs and strained to see what was causing all the excitement, but he couldn't see anything. Mama allowed him to climb up onto her back for a better view, but his anxious eyes still saw nothing.

A beautiful rainbow spanned the sky above Beaver Tail Lake, but the poor cub couldn't see it. What a terrible way for him to find out that he had bad eyesight! All the other animals could see the rainbow, but why couldn't he? Mama Bear went back into the woods with a very sad cub trailing along behind her.

As time went by, the cub grew up, and like all young bears, he left his mama to fend for himself. As a matter of fact, he grew so much that he became the biggest bear in the whole Old North Woods, and everyone began calling him "Big Bear." He was also very strong, fast and smart. His only problem was his poor eyesight. This really bothered him, but he hoped that his tremendous height would help him see the next rainbow when it appeared. Patiently, he waited for the big day to arrive… and finally it did!

When word reached Big Bear's ears that a rainbow had arrived, he raced straight down to the meadow near Beaver Tail Lake. Other animals were already there, and they were celebrating under the beautiful brilliant colors that stretched across the sky. Big Bear stood as tall as he could, and looked for the rainbow, but he couldn't find it. He rubbed his small eyes with his huge paws and tried again, but it was no use; he still could not see the rainbow. Everyone around him was happy, and this frustrated Big Bear even more. He grew very, very angry. In a fit of rage, Big Bear gave a terrible roar that seemed to shake everything in the Old North Woods! Animals scattered this way and that, trying to hide themselves as Big Bear tore up the meadow and threw huge rocks at the sky. Then, after giving one last gigantic roar, Big Bear headed up the mountainside to be alone.

Big Bear wandered aimlessly for days until he found a lonely dark cave near the banks of a fast-flowing river. Knowing that he was no longer welcome in the area near Beaver Tail Lake, he decided to make this cave his new home. He hoped that no one would ever find him there and that he would never hear the word "rainbow" again!

 Seasons came and went, and Big Bear grew old and lonely. His only companions were dozens of bats that shared the cave with him. They never said much as they hung on the walls, but they always seemed to be happy. Every night, they would fly off into the darkness to feast on insects, and every morning, before daylight, they would return to the cave to sleep away the day. Most of them had never even seen the sun, and one day it occurred to Big Bear that, like him, none of them had ever seen a rainbow!

Ah! So you see that it was not by chance that Big Bear had found that cave. Nor was it by chance that it was full of happy creatures that had eyesight worse than him! The Great Creator had been at work in Big Bear's life, and now, at last, he finally understood that one of the smallest creatures had taught one of the biggest a very valuable lesson - the lesson of what contentment means.

Big Bear asked the Great Creator for

forgiveness. He was sorry that he had let his poor eyesight make him blind to all the wonderful things the Great Creator had given him. He remembered that at one time he had been strong and fast. He also thought of his loving Mama Bear who had raised him, and the beautiful woods where he lived. He realized that he had wasted much of his life being bitter instead of being thankful. Big Bear knew what he had to do. He had to go back down to the meadow near Beaver Tail Lake, and say he was sorry to all the animals he had scared so long ago.

The river near Big Bear's cave flowed down through the meadow into Beaver Tail Lake, so Big Bear decided to follow it. As he was moving along it began to rain and the dampness made his creaky old bones ache. Soon, he hurt so badly that he had to stop and rest on a sand bar next to the river. The Great Creator had been watching the whole time, and had heard Big Bear's prayer asking for forgiveness. He also knew that Big Bear wouldn't be able to go on any farther.

Suddenly, a wonderful, warm breeze parted the clouds, and the rain stopped. The golden sun jumped out of hiding and a glorious rainbow leaped across Beaver Tail Lake. Only this time, the Great Creator caught the rainbow and threw it down into Beaver Tail Lake! This so startled a school of trout that they swam out of the lake and up into the river. The frightened fish swam so hard and far that they eventually rounded the same bend where Big Bear was resting.

At first, Big Bear's tired old eyes barely opened at the sound of splashing fish. But then his eyes burst open wide at the amazing scene before him. He could see a rainbow! The trout had carried the rainbow up

the river to him! Big Bear grinned a great big bear grin as the beautifully colored fish leaped and splashed everywhere. Each one was painted with its own multi-colored rainbow. It was the most beautiful thing he had ever seen… and he was very happy.

Just before Big Bear's eyes closed into the deepest of all sleeps, he asked the Great Creator for one last favor. Could He possibly leave the rainbow colored fish in the stream to remind those who saw them to be thankful for all of His wonderful gifts?

Amazingly, at that moment, somewhere down on Beaver Tail Lake, the Prayer Bird stopped what she was doing, because she felt compelled to sing…and so she did!

…And so it is, to this very day, that rainbow trout swim the cold, clear waters of the Old North Woods, bringing an unexpected "bear-like grin" to all who see them.

…Let your lives overflow with thanksgiving
for all he has done.
Colossians 2:7

Chapter 5

The Dead Tree Valley

Way back in a time that only the ancient trees remember, there was a lonely little valley in the Old North Woods. All of its trees had mysteriously died, and they stood like skeleton guards, silently warning any who thought about entering to stay away. The creatures of the forest felt that curses of drought,

42

disease, and death lay beyond the trees' posts, so the valley remained abandoned. It seemed like the Great Creator had turned His back on this part of His creation, which was so unlike Him. Such was the mystery of the Dead Tree Valley.

High above the valley, on a forested ridge, resided a colony of porcupines, otherwise known to the more knowledgeable nature lover as a 'prickle' of porcupines. Their den, which was in a hollow tree, was hardly big enough for all of them. One particular member was getting very tired of the poking she got every time someone tried to move. Sharp quills are wonderful for defending oneself against an enemy, but not so good for family and friends in tight quarters.

Something else was bothering her as well. Nothing about her life ever changed. Day after day, she'd climb down from the den, find a tree with some good bark, eat some bark, and then go back to the den to get poked some more. She saw nothing special about herself, or her dull life. Something had to change, because she felt she would die of boredom!

One day, while she sat on a boring tree limb, chewing yet another boring mouthful of bark, she heard a loud noise that was not boring at all. It came from down in the Dead Tree Valley, and it sounded like wild, uncontrolled laughter! The rhythm and pitch of it constantly changed, as if the mind of the one doing the laughing wasn't quite 'right.'

"Kuk-kuk…kuk-kuk…kuk-kuk-kuk-kuk-kuk!"

Then there was another equally strange sound, the sound of someone, or something, drumming on a tree or fallen log. This also lacked any thought-out cadence, which again suggested that the one responsible was a bit odd.

"Tap…tap-tap-tap-tap
…thump-thump
…tap-tap-tap-tap-tap!"

The wide-eyed porcupine waddled back to her den with the exciting news. It turned out that the others had heard the unusual sounds as well, and the porcupines unanimously concluded that some poor soul had dared to enter the Dead Tree Valley, and now they were under a curse of insanity. There was nothing that could be done that wouldn't doom a would-be rescuer, so all agreed to continue their daily lives at a very safe distance.

As the days passed, the crazy sounds from the valley continued. Sometimes the laughing and drumming would end with the sound of a tree crashing to the ground. This really aroused the curiosity of the porcupine. She desperately wanted to know what was going on among those dead trees. She also desperately longed for an adventure. Finally, she could stand it no more, and these words burst from her mouth, "There is an unsolved mystery, and I am going to solve it! Just once, I'm going to step out of my safe and incredibly boring life, and enter into the exciting, heart-pounding world of the unknown!"

Saying this out loud was very liberating for her, and she wanted the others to feel the freshness of freedom as well. "Who will join me?" she asked her prickle of porkies, but none thought it wise. In fact, they all tried to talk her out of it, stating that if she entered the Dead Tree Valley she would be the next to lose her mind...or worse!

Her response was simple and direct, "I would rather lose my mind on a daring, worthwhile adventure, than to lose it sitting here doing nothing." Sensing her firm resolve, they had no recourse, but to wish her well, and to pray that the Great Creator would protect her.

She waited until mid-morning before heading down the ridge towards the valley, hoping she might be less scared in the bright daylight. Word had traveled fast, and all along the way, woodland animals silently watched her pass. Some looked down and shook their heads, already mourning the loss of a poor, misguided friend. Such votes of confidence made her first attempt at epic bravery feel more like a march of doom. Still, she marched on.

The rising morning breeze brought the strong smell of rotten wood to her nostrils. She was almost there, and her steps slowed as the trees came clearly into view. She was all alone now, and she felt every bit of it.

As she walked beneath the first of the dead trees, the quills on her rump and stubby tail stood up straight, and her breathing quickened. Ghostly holes in the tree trunks formed lifelike mouths and eyes with unchanging expressions of agony. She was certain the trees were about to grab her with their brittle, pale-gray limbs. Oh, how she longed for the safety of her crowded little den. Even so, she refused to turn back.

As she made her way along, she passed between two large trees that seemed to have been staring at each other when they passed away. While quite frightening, she also felt it was somewhat romantic. It was as if they had been gazing into each other's eyes when they left this world for the next. She wondered if, at one time, their canopies had even embraced. She was a sentimental creature, and in honor of such a love, she thought it would be nice to let one sad tear escape from the corner of her eye.

Unfortunately, both the solemn tear, and the romantic moment were lost, because the two trees started laughing! It was the same terrible laughter she had heard while up on the ridge, only now it was a more hollow sound. Of course, the porcupine did what all porcupines do when startled. She turned her back to the threatening trees and bristled her spines. With her eyes closed tight, she braced herself for the assumed painful ending of her life. This only made the two trees laugh harder, and much louder.

When the laughter ended, the two trees began to speak. One said, "Look here, we finally have a guest, and it's a porcupine!" to which the other replied, "I once had a friend that was a porcupine. He was a little pokey, but a real stickler for punctuality!" With that, they both began laughing all over again.

Sensing that she was taking the situation far too seriously, the porcupine opened her eyes, relaxed her quills, and turned around to face the trees again. Right away, she noticed that the mouths of both trees appeared to have brilliant red tongues. She could also see that these 'tongues' had a set of eyes and a beak beneath them! Realizing that she had been the victim of humorous trickery, she insisted, "Whoever you are, come out of those holes!"

Without hesitation, a large and strikingly elegant bird climbed out of the mouth of each tree. Both displayed a beautiful black suit of feathers, with bold white stripes on their necks and faces. A flaming red 'tongue-like' crest of feathers stood erect upon their heads. The male wore a touch more red on his head than the female, and he sported a dashing red mustache as well. The porcupine could hardly imagine a more handsome couple in all of the Old North Woods. Nor could she imagine how such an attractive bird could laugh in such an unattractive way. Today we would recognize these birds as a mating pair of pileated woodpeckers, but back then, they were incredibly rare and unfamiliar birds.

Both birds landed on a log and exchanged proper greetings with the porcupine, and then they talked and talked as if they had been her best friends forever. The longer she remained in the company of the good-natured pair, the more she fell in love with

them. She could not stop laughing at their jokes, or at the fact that she had once been afraid of them. She learned that the drumming she heard came from the strong strikes of their heavy bills on rotten wood. They told her that their favorite food in the whole world was the carpenter ants that they had discovered in the Dead Tree Valley.

Every so often, the birds dug their holes so deep that a tree would break in half and fall to the ground. This was all starting to make sense to the porcupine. The mysteries of the Dead Tree Valley were not so mysterious any more.

Finally, there was only one difficult question left to answer, and the brave porcupine asked it, "For what good reason have all these trees died?" The woodpeckers smiled warmly and moved closer to each other. Then one of them answered with a very gentle whisper, "Perhaps they died so that we could live." At that, the porcupine looked up again at the two trees who, even in death, still gazed lovingly at one another. She then found the tear that she had lost earlier. She knew that she would never see the Dead Tree Valley, or her life, the same way again. It seemed that in some way, the dead trees had given her a wonderful gift as well. Maybe the Great Creator hadn't turned His back on this valley after all. Could it be that death has no power to end what is truly good?

The days passed, and their friendship grew. The porcupine introduced the prickle to her two new friends, and because of their wonderful woodpecker humor, things were never, ever boring again. They even tasted new foods together, and while the

 porcupines never developed a taste for ants or termites, the woodpeckers discovered that the choke cherries growing on the ridge were an excellent dessert. The woodpeckers even carved out several new dens for the porcupines, solving the problem of over-crowding. The birds enjoyed doing this act of good will so much that they are still making shelters for other animals to this day, and their crazy laughter fills the forest air while they are doing it.

Friends, life is full of difficult tragedies that we all must find a way to endure. For some, it is most comforting to hear the mournful cry of the Prayer Bird on a quiet night. For others, the healing comes with unexpected laughter… laughter that can only come from a mysteriously joyful Spirit. It is comforting to know that the Great Creator lovingly provides both, the loon and the woodpecker, to those who would listen for them.

And I am convinced that nothing
can ever separate us from his love.
Death can't, and life can't.
The angels can't, and the demons can't.
Our fears for today, our worries about tomorrow,
And even the powers of hell
can't keep God's love away.
Romans 8:38

Chapter 6

A True and Mighty Ruler

Way back in a time that only the ancient trees remember, two mighty birds ruled the skies over the Old North Woods. The Great Creator himself had given them this high honor, and it was his Spirit's breath that helped them glide effortlessly amongst the clouds.

Born from the same nest, the two birds looked very much alike, but deep down beneath their shiny black feathers they were not alike at all. The sister bird's heart was happiest when she was near water, and it beat with the purpose to serve others. But the brother bird's heart was most pleased over the land, and it beat to be served. And so it was, that for a time both humility and pride governed over the creatures below, and all would bow at the passing of their majestic shadows.

Of course, this season of compromise was bound to end…and it did, on one dreadful day of testing.

It seemed as if the sun never rose that day. It was like it had been rudely pushed aside by legions of black and angry clouds that marched in from the east. All creation shook as the invaders beat their terrible thunder drums. The storm's assault on the Old North Woods was so swift and aggressive that there was little time to prepare. A mighty wall of wind and rain swept across the land, snapping trees and flooding streams as it passed. Terrified animals scurried to find whatever shelter they could. Even the two "mighty rulers of the skies" sought a place of refuge. Instinctively they both flew to the tallest and strongest white pine tree on Beaver Tail Lake. This was the place of their birth - their nesting tree.

Oddly, choosing the same tree to ride out the storm was about all the two had in common anymore. Enduring each other could prove to be as difficult as enduring the storm. They said nothing as they clutched a limb and awkwardly huddled together. After a brief glance at one another, they both tucked their heads beneath their wings and prepared themselves for a very long and miserable day.

It was while they were perched there together that they both heard something. Somehow, even over the mighty roar of the wind, the sound of the waves crashing, and the rain hitting the water, they could detect the sound of gulls crying somewhere down the distant shoreline. "What were gulls doing out in a storm such as this?" they wondered.

Sister Bird withdrew her head from under her wing and squinted in the direction of the calling. She could barely make out a huge flock of gulls hovering and circling and diving upon a cluster of near-shore boulders. No, these birds weren't feeding. Not even a fool bird would try to feed today. Something must be wrong!

Sister Bird nudged her brother and said, "We should look into this situation. Someone could be in trouble." But her brother kept his head beneath his wing and mumbled, "If gulls wish to risk their lives playing around on a day like today that's their business... we must protect ourselves." "No!" Sister

Bird insisted, "With the honor that has been given us comes certain duties. We must offer our help!" And with that, she leaped up into the wind. Brother Bird gave a disgusted sigh and reluctantly followed.

As the pair drew near, the desperate squawking of hundreds of gulls became deafening. Looking down through the chaotic swarm of frantic birds revealed the source of their misery: a lone white bird was trapped amongst the jagged black rocks. Somehow he had managed to get his foot stuck in a crack, and no amount of pulling and struggling was getting it free.

To make matters worse, it seemed as if all the forces of nature were conspiring to destroy the bird. The winds were blowing harder and harder. The waves were growing bigger and bigger. Each wave took its turn to beat down their helpless victim. The poor bird tried to catch its breath between each pounding, but the waves were coming too fast. His strength was fading and his comrades wailed in distress. Any that tried to rescue their friend risked being thrown into the rocks by the next wave. It was a miserable situation indeed!

At some point one of the gulls looked up and recognized the two large birds circling above. Sensing that there could be some hope, it cried out, "Help him!

Help him!" This in turn, got the rest of the flock's attention, so they all began to cry, "Help him! Help him!" Brother Bird was quick to answer back, "What can we do that hasn't already been tried? And whose responsibility is this anyway? These rocks are not part of my territory, nor are they truly part of my sister's!"

Meanwhile, Sister Bird had no excuses. Every wave that pounded the small white bird was punishing her heart as well. There was no time to rethink what needed to be done. The Great Creator had given her the tools to do what had to be done. Her whole life had prepared her for this moment. She could stand it no longer...so she dove! Brother Bird cried out to stop her, "There will always be more gulls! It's not worth it Sister!" But she just picked up speed as she dropped towards the earth.

The throng of birds separated as she knifed down through them. Wind and rain tried to stop her. Yet she kept her eyes on her target. Timing was everything. She had to land between the waves and do her work quickly.

It happened so fast.
Talons hit.
Her beak did what it was designed to do.
And crimson flowed.

Just before the biggest and angriest of all the waves hit those rocks, she could be seen standing over the gulls' limp body...with her head and tail cupped down over him...and her wings outstretched...ready to take the blow.

It hit like a crack of thunder,
and then both were gone.

Having completed its mission, the storm immediately ceased, and all was calm. The gulls landed and began to search the rocks. Brother Bird searched from the air, and he was the first to spot them. A short distance away the birds had washed up together on a sandy beach.

But was it really them?

For you see, neither one looked the same any more. The gull was now missing a leg, and for some reason he looked whiter, and more magnificent than he had ever looked before! And Sister Bird had gained beautiful royal white feathers on both her head and tail! Better yet, somehow they were both alive! As they began to help each other up, a great celebration of rejoicing began, and of course the gulls were noisier than ever! It took quite a while for things to calm down before someone could speak. But when things finally did, it wasn't one of the two "mighty rulers of the skies" that spoke. Instead, it was the one-legged gull who spoke, and when he did, it was with the voice of The Great Creator!

This is what He said:

"Today we have witnessed a wonderful thing, a selfless act that revealed the heart of a true and mighty ruler. Her servanthood has gained her a feathered crown. From this day on, Sister Bird's generations will grow to appear as she does, and they will rule the skies forever."

Of course, such a wonderful proclamation deserved a high-spirited call from the Prayer Bird, who was out near the middle of the lake. This, in turn, aroused all creatures within earshot to join in the cheering.

We all might wish that this was the end of this story… but unfortunately, it's not. Brother Bird was stricken with a terrible fit of anger and jealousy. He wanted the rewards his sister had received. He claimed to have been tricked by The Great Creator. He complained, "How was I to know that a gull stuck in the rocks was really The Great Creator?" He even went on to say, "If deception is what it takes to become great…then a deceiver is who I will be!"

So in an effort to look like his sister, he flew back to the nesting tree, broke off a branch, and let the sap run down upon his head. Sure enough, as the sap hardened, his head turned white! For a while he was pleased. But then the sticky mass upon his head began to itch. Eventually, the itching became so bad that he landed on the ground to rub his head on a large rock. Can you imagine his embarrassment when his head became glued to that rock?

Ironically, it was Sister Bird who heard his calls for help and came to his rescue. The process of removing the sap was long and painful. It also involved

the removal of all Brother Bird's head feathers! To this day, Brother Bird's family is unable to grow

feathers on their heads, which begs the humorous question: Why don't we call our vultures "bald" instead of our eagles?   Furthermore, even today we can witness the curse of this species' continued pride, since they are no longer allowed to be rulers over living creatures...only the dead can be seen bowing mindlessly before them.

Finally...in order to end on a more pleasant thought...please take notice the next time you walk along a beach...that you might enjoy counting how many gulls are standing on one leg. This is in honor of the day that The Great Creator came down and became one of them!

And the King will tell them, 'I assure you,
when you did it to one of the
least of these my brothers and sisters,
you were doing it to me!'
Matthew 25:40

Chapter 7

The Otter and Mr. Blue

Way back in a time that only the ancient trees remember, a great blue heron hunted and fished the

64

calm waters of a bayou in the Old North Woods. This very tall bird had very long legs, a very long neck, and a very long face. He could even stand perfectly still for a very long time, which is what he often did while waiting for his next meal to come hopping, swimming or crawling along. It seemed everything about him was very long, except for one thing: his patience for others. Unfortunately, that was very short! He was often heard squawking harshly as he flew away from a backwater neighbor who had accidentally gotten too close while trying to be friendly.

As always, the Great Creator had been watching. He knew the needs of that grumpy old bird's heart, so He asked the Prayer Bird to make a call for a very special servant…

Things got started early in the morning, with a plump bullfrog swimming slowly along the bank of the bayou. It had no idea that with each lazy kick of its legs it was coming closer to becoming a meal! For there, high above the water was the statue-like form of the great blue heron. Its neck was slightly pulled back, like a bow being held at full draw. Any second, his arrow-like beak would fly

forward in a blur of motion, and the frog would be his! So intense was the heron's

concentration on the frog that he no longer heard the squabbling red winged blackbirds in the cattails.

He no longer saw the dragonfly hovering just over his head who, by the way, was hoping to see that "long-tongued, bug-eater-of-a-frog" become a lump in the heron's throat! No, not even the commotion of a big ol' river otter belly- sliding down the bank was noticed. Well… at least not until it was discovered that big ol' belly-sliding otters do not fit between the legs of wading blue herons!

KER-SPLASH!

The explosion of water, feathers, mud and weeds, was immediately followed by a whole lot of coughing and squawking. The normally dignified and well-groomed bird was now an awful, smelly mess, and very angry! The otter, on the other hand, seemed rather unscathed by the whole ordeal. Actually, he was very amused by it! His playful chuckling did nothing to help the heron's foul mood. Neither did comments like: "Sorry! I guess your breakfast will live to CROAK another day!" The otter floated on his back and wiped a laughter tear away as the mighty bird re-erected himself, one towering section at a time, and then taking a moment to shake his feathers dry. After calming himself down, the heron's stern stare fell upon the otter, and his only words were, "GO AWAY!" But it was as if the words had completely missed the otter's

really small ears, because he replied, "I like you, Mr. Blue. You make me laugh! I think I shall be your best friend!"

The frustrated bird objected to the idea of being called "Mr. Blue," and to having acquired a new "best friend," but it didn't matter…from that day on, the otter made daily visits to "cheer up" Mr. Blue. And of course, he always showed up at exactly the worst possible time, said the wrong things, and was a great distraction to the bird's otherwise peaceful and quiet life…

Like the spring day that the otter introduced Mr. Blue to the backwater's biggest and orneriest dogfish by proudly announcing, "I've seen my feathered friend eat fifty of those cute little fry in one meal!" Or the dreadful calm day that neither came close to catching a meal because of all the disgusting sounds and smells coming from an otter who had spent the whole night at an 'all-you-can-eat clam buffet.' Actually, the only time it seemed Mr. Blue truly appreciated the otter's spirit-lifting efforts was when the furry fellow brought him a quartet of spring peeper frogs to sing him happy birthday. Much to the otter's dismay, the plump heron was listening to a solo before the last note was sung!

Without a doubt, a stranger pair could not have been found in all of the Old North Woods.

The years passed, and the otter and Mr. Blue grew old together. Not much between the two changed. Mr. Blue remained just as grouchy as the day they met, and the otter continued to be his ever smiling, "best friend." This completely baffled the other bayou animals. They would frequently ask the otter, "Why don't you give up on that old bird? He's never going to change! Can't you see that he'll never like anybody?" To this, the otter always replied, "I like Mr. Blue. He makes me laugh!" Not even the wisest owl could convince the otter to give up his loyalty to the one-sided relationship.

Age took its toll, and both the otter and Mr. Blue were slowing down and finding it harder to catch a meal. Fish seemed to swim much faster than they used to. Mr. Blue noticed that the otter had even given up the silly habit of playing with his food before he ate it. And the otter noticed that every morning, at first light, Mr. Blue seemed to have trouble catching his first fish. He wondered if "Old Blue's" eyes were beginning to fail him. The end result was always a dropped fish. Hating to see a stunned bluegill or bass go to waste, the otter would slide in and help himself to the escapee. After downing the tasty morsel, the otter would tease his friend with something like, "Now would you look at that, you DO have a soft heart...such a delicious gift you've given me!" Of course, Mr. Blue would grumble about it for a while, and then try to ignore the otter while he resumed fishing.

The day finally came when Mr. Blue no longer hunted and fished the calm waters of the bayou. Sadly, no one but the otter and the crying Prayer Bird seemed to care that he was missing. The otter grieved the loss of his friend deeply. It broke his heart that after all their time together he had failed to fix that grumpy old bird's heart. There was no laughter behind his otter tears now. After climbing out of the water up onto a log, he took a moment and started to say he was sorry to the Great Creator for not getting the job done, but the Great Creator interrupted him by simply whispering:

"Watch..."

At that moment, a much younger great blue heron glided in and landed in the shallows. The bird looked remarkably similar to the otter's old friend as it stood there, statue still, with its neck pulled slightly back. It waited...then, in an instant, its arrow-like beak shot forward and sliced through the water. Catching fish looked easy for this magnificent creature. Yet for some reason, in the process of preparing to swallow the fish, it was dropped! The otter couldn't believe that a heron so young and so agile could be so clumsy. As the injured fish floated by, the otter was compelled to ask, "Excuse me young fellow...why is it that you dropped this first fish of the morning?" The bird looked surprised by the question, and hesitated before replying, "I'm not sure, it's just something Grandpa Blue taught me to do."

With that, the otter chuckled and said,
"I like you, young Mr. Blue.
You make me laugh!"

Some things never change, perhaps because there's purpose in it. To this day, otters are still carefree, happy-go-lucky animals who just can't help but put a smile on anyone's face. Likewise, great blue herons still appear intolerant and grumpy. They'll grumble, squawk, and fly away if you happen to disturb their fishing. But before you judge them on such things, bear in mind, there are long-standing traditions to uphold in the Old North Woods... traditions that might hide a heron's smile, and what truly lies within his heart.

"...The LORD doesn't make decisions the way you do!
People judge by outward appearance,
But the LORD looks at a person's
thoughts and intentions."
I Samuel 16:7

Chapter 8

The King and His Crown

Way back in a time that only the ancient trees remember, there lived an enormous moose in the Old North Woods. No other animal compared to him in size or strength. The ground shook when he walked, and his head alone was as big as a bear! He had fiery eyes, and steam came from his huge nostrils. He knew no fear because he was the King of the swamp.

To be a king, one has to have a crown, and every year the King would grow one. His "crown" was a massive set of antlers, and every year they seemed to get bigger. Broad and heavy, and adorned with many dagger-like points, the King would use his antlers to destroy trees, which then marked the boundaries of his kingdom in the swamp. No one dared to enter and challenge him, not even the wolves.

But then, each and every winter something mysterious happened. The King's crown would fall off! This greatly upset him. He would paw the ground and grunt, "how can a king rule without his crown?!" He knew the Great Creator was responsible for his antlers falling off, and he didn't understand why, nor did he like it. Worse yet, he thought the wolves would find out and not fear him anymore. And since the King ran from no one, he might have to fight without his best defensive weapon. Knowing this just made him angrier.

Eventually, it happened one summer's day, while the King was admiring the reflection of his new and growing set of antlers in a lily pool, that he made a decision. He decided that he would never give up his crown. He vowed to keep his big and beautiful antlers where they belonged... on his head! A warning cry from the Prayer Bird found its way across Beaver Tail Lake, and then into the swamp...but he ignored it.

Of course, no moose has the right to think such things, even if they are the King of the swamp. But surprisingly, the Great Creator allowed this stubborn, prideful moose to have his way. As a matter of fact, the

Great Creator even caused his antlers to grow faster than normal to an unbelievable size! Needless to say, the King was very pleased, even if they were a bit awkward and heavy. Later, when his magnificent crown remained on his head well into the dead of winter, the proud king strutted around his swamp, bellowing and tearing up the trees.

As the days passed, the snow continued to fall. The drifts were getting deeper and deeper. It was even getting difficult for a long-legged moose to move around. Food was becoming scarce. And for the first time in his life, the King felt his strength beginning to leave him. He bedded down more often, usually with his head in the snow. This was done in order to take the weight of his antlers off his neck. Yes, the king's "crown" had become a heavy burden.

Then he heard it: the hungry howl of a wolf! Soon it was joined by another…and another. The King knew that the pack was on the hunt, and that this time they were coming after him! They sensed his weakness, and had been waiting a long time for this opportunity. The fire had left his eyes, and even with his crown, he no longer felt like a king.

The tired giant rose to his feet. Not to face his enemies, but to run! Instinctively, he knew that the deep, open water of the river was his only chance. It was there that his long legs would give him the advantage over the wolves, because they wouldn't be able to touch bottom. So with all the strength that he could muster, he ran for the river!

It was hard going for the poor fellow as he plowed his way through chest-deep snow. Meanwhile, the much lighter wolves ran across the top of the packed snow and were gaining ground quickly. No longer did they follow him with their noses... through the blowing snow, they could see him!

The river was within sight now, but the moose was exhausted and slowing down. He knew that he wasn't going to make it. He also knew that it was the weight of his crown that doomed him. So he resigned himself to one final prayer to his Great Creator:

"Take my crown, and my cursed pride with it!"

And with that, in an instant, his antlers fell off!

With the great weight removed from his head, the moose found renewed strength and was able to press on. At the same time, the wolves came upon the antlers in the snow and momentarily thought that the King had fallen. They pounced upon them, but found no moose! Only then did they realize that they had been fooled, and that the King was now facing them, standing knee deep in the river! Steam was coming from his nostrils and the fire had returned to his eyes. No wolf dared to enter the water and face his sharp hooves.

The next spring, the cycle began again, with two small fuzzy antlers appearing on his head. The King had no idea how big his crown would grow, nor how long he would have it...but that no longer mattered. Those things were for the Great Creator to decide...and a very good reason for the Prayer Bird to sing!

**So humble yourselves
under the mighty power of God,
and in his good time he will honor you.
I Peter 5:6**

Chapter 9

The Most Magnificent
Oak Possum

Way back in a time that only the ancient trees remember, there grew a grove of 13 oak trees in the heart of the Old North Woods. Straight and tall they stood, like stately columns of a glorious temple. When entering the cool shade of their canopy, the animals knew they were in a special place. Out of respect for these giants, even the noisiest of woodland critters hushed themselves to a whisper. Many even felt some kind of magic in the air when they came near those old trees. This was particularly true when they found themselves at the foot of the grandest of the 13… "The Most Magnificent Oak." It was under this famous tree that this tale begins.

Harvest season was over in the oak grove. The animals of the forest had enjoyed their annual feast of large, sweet tasting acorns. Nearby hollow trees, logs, and holes in the ground were all full to overflowing in preparation for the long, cold winter. Only a few overlooked nuts lay widely scattered on the ground, and by this time no one considered it worth looking for them.

Well… almost no one.

In the stillness of a frosty morning, as first light began to reveal the many different forms and shapes of the forest, an odd figure entered the scene. Brittle leaves rustled and crunched as the small possum waddled about looking for leftovers. No glorious words like 'beautiful' or 'elegant' could possibly be used to describe her appearance. Instead, only polite words such as 'unique' or 'interesting' might be used. This was in hopes of avoiding the embarrassing potential of offending her or her creator. She had patchy gray and white fur, a wet, pointy nose, and a long, hairless tail

Her small, thin ears were torn and jagged from fights and frostbite. She also had sharp claws for climbing trees and for getting her way.

Being a scavenger her whole life had not been easy, and her heart, much like her ears, had paid the price with scars. It had been a long time since love or kindness had put food in her belly. Instead, she had survived by being mean... but her heart was tired of the wounds, and now she just wanted to be alone. This is why she waited until after the harvest to come to the grove. No one would be there to whisper bad things about her, or to ignore her, or bully her. Only the oaks would be there, and she liked the oaks, because they never judged her.

Eventually, all her sniffing and scratching and digging around in the leaves brought her into the presence of The Most Magnificent Oak. Her eyes traveled from the gnarled roots that pushed up through the earth, upwards along the furrowed, gray trunk, where massive branches extended like mighty arms holding up the sky. She had climbed many trees during her lifetime, but never this one or any of the others in the grove. She felt unworthy to touch them. Something caught her eye as her gaze dropped back down to her world below. A glimmer of light was reflecting off an object that was hanging off a branch.

'Could it be?' She thought.

'Yes! One acorn remained on the tree!'

Her whole life, she had heard stories about those who had the good fortune of discovering the last acorn of the season. Since no other acorn would fall after it, the last was said to have magical powers. The excited possum could hardly breathe. She could not believe that she was actually looking up at a magic acorn...and better yet... that it was hanging from a branch of The Most Magnificent Oak! The king of all oaks! She wondered about the incredible powers held between that cap and shell, and about how she could use those powers.

Of course, every good thing comes with rules, and all the animals of the Old North Woods knew the two simple rules for obtaining the magic from the last acorn of the season:

Rule #1: The acorn must fall on its own, when it is ready, with no help.

Rule #2: The acorn's magic belongs only to the first one who picks it up. If it is eaten, set aside, dropped, or given away, it loses its power.

Our little possum friend found herself in an unusual situation. Being good and following the rules had never worked for her. Could she really let this little seed become her master? Could she really wait there until it was ready to fall? What would happen if someone else came along and saw her guarding the last acorn of the season that just happened to be hanging from The Most Magnificent Oak? Would she have to fight for it? No, she could not fight. The grove of oaks was a sacred place, even for scoundrels such as herself.

She needed a plan. So she thought about it for a while… and then, for a while longer. Then, all at once she smiled a wide possum grin, because she had come up with a plan, and a good plan it was! She would pretend to be dead. Then she could lay under the tree and keep an eye on the acorn. Meanwhile, anyone else who passed by would be so busy looking at the poor 'dead' possum they would fail to look up and notice the acorn. She chuckled at how smart she was as she looked for a comfortable spot to 'die.' Upon finding a soft bed of leaves directly beneath the dangling treasure, she flopped onto her back and stuck her tongue out of the corner of her foamy mouth.

So there she lay, motionless, as the sun traveled through the tree branches above her. No animals came. Still, she was determined to stick with her plan.

The sun continued to play its game of hide-n-seek with her. When it went behind a tree branch, it got dark. When it came out from behind the branch, it got so bright that she had to close her eyes. On and on it went. Dark…bright…dark…bright…dark…bright. The last thing she remembered thinking was it sure was tiresome being dead!

She awoke to a small twig hitting her on the nose. She had twitched as her eyes popped open and hoped that no one had seen. Another twig fell, this one just missing her ear. She held very still. By the time a third twig bounced off her shoulder she had spied the source. There, perched on the same branch that **her** acorn dangled from, was the black silhouette of a crow with a twig in his beak!

Her prize had been discovered!

Fortunately, even with one last twig dropping squarely onto her chest, she had remained 'dead' enough to fool the bird. He clearly no longer saw her as a threat as he relaxed and turned his attention to the acorn. Anger welled up within her as she thought about this villain taking what was hers. She had dealt with crows before and had no good feelings for them. Many a time she had felt pain from their beaks as she fought them for scraps of leftover food. She was sure that he, of all creatures, had no place being in The Most Magnificent Oak. Even so, she remained 'dead,' knowing that the element of surprise would work in her favor.

Both waited.

As daylight began to fade, a cool breeze from the high places swept through the grove. As it passed, the acorn gently rocked under its limb… and then, it let go. Desperate anticipation seemed to magically freeze both bird and beast into statues. The spell was broken when the nut thumped on the ground.

The crow was caught off-guard by the sudden movement of the 'dead' possum. He fell from his perch and spiraled awkwardly to the ground, crashing into the leaves. The possum was upon the acorn before her rival could even rise to his feet. 'Something is wrong,' she thought. It was too easy to beat him.

She made her first wish as she held the prize close to her heart.

The crow gained his footing and shook the dirt from his bill. Upon seeing that he had lost, he sighed and turned to leave, dragging his crippled wing behind him.

She understood now. The crow had come to The Most Magnificent Oak to ask it for healing. He had seen the last acorn of the season and thought it was a gift for him! It must have taken a lot of effort for him to climb the tree while attempting to get out of sight as he waited for the acorn to fall. Only after he had climbed the tree did he notice the possum down below. Imagine his relief when his dropped twigs proved that she was dead. But he was fooled...and now his relief had turned to hopelessness and his wing was in worse shape than before. Such was the life of a good-for-nothing-crow.

But wait...a whisper was heard.

"Please stop."

He turned to see her waddling towards him. Rising on her hind legs, she removed the acorn from her newly wished-for pocket. This pocket, hidden on her stomach, would have prevented her from ever needing to set the acorn down. She could have magical powers for the rest of her life! Yet, she held the acorn out to him.

"This will never work," he said.

"Take it anyway," she replied.

As he took the acorn in his beak, against all the rules, his wing and her heart were both healed! Flapping his strong wings and leaping into the air, the overjoyed crow dropped the acorn down to his new friend and loudly proclaimed, "May the Great Creator bless you for what you have done, Most Magnificent Oak Possum!" Then he flew up and away... much farther up and away than anyone had ever been.

It seemed as if her heart was flying in the clouds with the crow as she danced below. Her burden of guilt disappeared when he did, and the old possum was gone. A new creature walked the forest floor in that scoundrel's place, and her name was "The Most Magnificent Oak Possum!"

Before she left the grove of oaks, she dug a hole and gently placed the acorn in it. She smiled as she pulled a warm blanket of earth over it and vowed to protect it. Now she knew that the healing had not come from the acorn, or even the oak. A much greater power, of goodness, and grace, had been at work…the same kind of power that makes a seed grow and the dead come back to life. Only the Great Creator has that kind of power!

Regretfully, over the years, the name "Most Magnificent Oak Possum" has faded to "Magnificent Oak Possum," then to "Oak Possum," and finally shortened to what we have today, with a few folks calling her an "Opossum," and the rest calling her a "possum" again. Perhaps it would be good if we remembered her whole name once again. Perhaps it would be good if we all plopped an acorn in our own pocket to help us remember that The Great Creator can be big or small…and that on one special day He chose to be very small… small enough to enter an acorn and a wounded heart.

To this day, all "Most Magnificent Oak Possums" play dead rather than fight, and the females still have a pocket, which they now use to carry their acorn sized young… and somewhere in the Old North Woods, 14 giant oaks grow, and the Prayer Bird calls as she wings southward overhead.

He heals the brokenhearted,
binding up their wounds.
Psalm 147:3

Chapter 10

Fireball

Way back in a time that only the ancient trees remember, there was an amazing place where blue waves from vast waters hit the shore and turned into golden swells of sand. Pushed by persistent winds, and rolling ever so slowly inland, these dunes increased in size and carried with them green caps of tall grass and splashes of low-growing juniper. Occasionally, clumps of jack and white pine were able to anchor themselves in low-lying swales, forming a shady oasis in an otherwise harsh environment. Only a few animals in the Old North Woods were able to survive in such a place. Because of their hardships, some drew closer to the Great Creator, while others turned their backs on Him. This is a story about both kinds of beast.

The first sounds of the summer morning were familiar to the little squirrel. Had we been in those pines, we would have heard something that sounded like a softly repeated "queedle, queedle," but what the squirrel actually heard was, "quick-in-the-needles, quick-in-the-needles." He dreaded this sound because he knew the Blue Jay Gang was heading his way. They flew from one prickly jack pine limb to another, scarcely staying longer than the blink of an eye in any one spot. Bright, sky-blue darts crossed openings faster than his eyes could follow, with empty bobbing limbs telling him where they had been.

It was just a matter of time before one of them found him, and then their call would immediately change to a disagreeably harsh, "JAY! JAY!" The routine was always the same...he would be surrounded by the flock

of proudly crested birds, each sporting identical black and white tattoos on their wings, tails and faces. Then the taunting would begin. Pinecones were stolen from his nest, and his favorite mushrooms, carefully hidden in the branches, were pecked to pieces and scattered on the ground. Wide-eyed and trembling, he would silently watch them from his branch, wondering if the Great Creator even cared that such things were going on. His fear turned to frustration and anger as the "quick-in-the-needles, quick-in-the-needles" chant resumed and the birds moved on in search of their next victim.

While it was true that he disliked the blue jays, he also envied them. They were handsomely bold while he was not. His drab gray fur and drooping tail seemed to match his personality. He was a slow and timid runt who could not scare a butterfly. He knew, because he had tried. Oh, the embarrassment of it all!

Then one hot afternoon, a rumbling came from over the waters. Flashes of light flickered in the sky and the squirrel grew nervous. He sought refuge in the hollow skeleton of a pine tree that had long ago lost its battle with the sand. From the security of an old woodpecker hole, he watched strings of lightning pull the dark clouds closer. Ahead of all the turmoil, he noticed a small, black, air-borne dot that progressively grew larger. Soon the dot turned into a strange, yet beautiful, black and white bird flying directly overhead. Stranger yet, was the call she made as she passed by, "Ha-oo-oo! Ha-oo-oo!" The long, haunting wail seemed to carry even more power than the storm behind it. It was then that he realized who the bird was. She was the wondrous loon that he'd heard tales of, the messenger of the Great Creator…it was the Prayer Bird! Her ghostly call scared the little fellow so badly that he fell back into the darkness of the tree and covered his ears. Most assuredly, that is what saved him from what happened next.

Unexpectedly, something other than his fear was making his fur stand on end! Suddenly a blinding light and deafening noise jolted him from his world into a world of dreams. It was a place where a small squirrel who looked exactly like him, wore regal red fur and was the beloved ruler of the pine forest. In this place, drab gray servant jays brought their squirrel-king fresh pinecones and mushrooms whenever he wanted to eat. He really liked this world, but his old world was calling him back.

Smoke filled his nose and burned his waking eyes. The lightning strike and subsequent fire had destroyed the hollow tree, but somehow he was alive! He stumbled away from a bed of hot coals and shook the ringing from his ears. He stroked his fur to remove the soot and redness from it, but it would not go away! His head, back, and tail were now a flaming red color, accented by a sleek, charcoal black racing stripe that ran down both sides of his body. His belly was lightning white, as was the fur around his eyes…and he liked it. He liked it a lot!

The other animals in the jack pine swale scarcely recognized him. Not only because of his changed appearance, but also his changed behavior. This new squirrel was a confident, look-you-in-the-eye, kind of squirrel that flicked his tail just to make sure he had your attention. He could move blazing fast in the trees and was a master of smack talk. He could say two dozen "don't mess with me" sentences without taking a breath, and he wasn't afraid to say them to anyone. And yes, he took great pleasure in scaring every butterfly that he saw!

The next morning the Blue Jay Gang never knew what hit them. A frightening red blur interrupted their usual "quick-in-the-needles, quick-in-the-needles" with a defiant chant of his own. It sounded a lot like this: "Stop-stop-stop-stop-stop-get-out-of-here! Stop-stop-

stop-stop-stop-scra-a-a-am!" This so startled the gang that they fumbled over their words and could only scream "JAY!" while something that looked like a fireball chased them from branch to branch, trying to burn their tail feathers! The flock scattered and they couldn't get out of those pines fast enough! It's no surprise that our little red friend was very pleased with himself and that he really liked it that his new friends had started to call him 'Fireball.' His only regret was that he had failed to scare the blue out of those jays!

It didn't take long for the glad news of Fireball's triumph over the widely disliked Blue Jay Gang to spread through the dunes. Most who heard the story believed that the Great Creator himself had been in the lightning bolt, and that He had changed the squirrel into a hero. Unfortunately, one very bad bobcat angrily refused to believe any part of that story. Her response to the news was to sharpen her claws on a stump and growl that she would have a red squirrel for breakfast!

Bobcats are notorious enemies of squirrels, but this one was the worst. She would pass up hunting for much easier prey, like mice or baby birds, if she knew that a squirrel was in the area. Just

smelling one put her on edge and made her mouth water. Knowing that there was a proud and disgustingly famous, pre-cooked meal in the area challenged her and made her insanely hungry! She did not care that this squirrel had any ties with the Great Creator, for her own ties with Him were long gone, lost, as if buried beneath the sun-scorched sands around her. If He would condemn her to live in the dunes, and could not, or would not, do a thing to make her life better, she saw no reason to revere Him. To her, the Great Creator was no better than a helpless squirrel that she had chased up a tree.

Night crept in and moonlight glistened on her mottled reddish-yellow coat as she circled the swale from high atop the dune. She knew Fireball was down there... sound asleep in his comfy little tree-hole nest. She would kill him in the morning, when he showed himself. For now, she would have some fun and make her intentions known. The stillness of the night was broken with these terrible, howling words: "I'll have the blood of a red squirrel in my whiskers! I'll have the blood of a **dead** squirrel in my whiskers!" The words echoed from dune to dune and into the nightmares of one poor little red squirrel.

Dawn found the bobcat up in a white pine, sniffing around the entrance hole of Fireball's empty nest. Her short, black-tipped tail twitched with delight when the smell of a hot trail entered her nostrils. It would be an easy trail to follow on the ground, even if the squirrel used the trees, because it reeked with panic. Her four paws hit the sand and she trotted off in silent pursuit.

Somewhere up ahead, our one-time-hero ran for his life. He leaped from tree to tree, ran through hollow logs, and even swam a shallow pond… all in an effort to throw the cat off his trail. Still she came, and he knew it. No squirrel could escape her, not even the mighty Fireball. Oh, how he wished that he had never heard the name Fireball! The Bobcat never knew he existed back when he was a nameless, slow moving, timid, runt. Why had the Great Creator done this to him? Soon, his cover of trees would thin out and there would be nothing but open sand. Certainly, being out in the open would mean his doom. Where could he go? What could he do?

In front of him, the bones of a lone tree stuck out of the crest of a dune. He thought to himself, 'This all started in a dead tree, why not end it in one as well?' With that in mind, Fireball scurried up the side of the hill and climbed to the very tip-top of the tree. There, panting, he awaited his executioner.

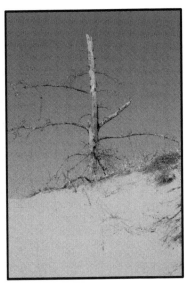

When the bobcat got to the opening and saw the squirrel high atop the tree, she slowed to a leisurely walk. The chase was over. Her piercing eyes never left him as she climbed the sand and then slowly circled the tree. "So! You are the mighty Fireball!" she taunted him. She continued, "Why don't you climb down here and teach me a lesson? Better yet, why don't you call down lightning and fire from above? I hear you are good at that!" Fireball was silent as he looked up into the clear blue sky. There would be no lightning today. Ah, but Fireball remembered a stronger power than what could be found in a storm. A power that had once both scared him and made him who he was. In desperation, he began to pray to the only one who could send such power...the Great Creator Himself.

It was then that he heard something.
A call, from far off in the distance.
"Ha-oo-oo! Ha-oo-oo!"

He opened his teary eyes and looked in the direction of the sound, and there it was! A small, black, air-borne dot was heading his way, and rapidly growing larger! The dot quickly turned into a familiar black and white bird flying directly overhead. She continued to call as she began to circle high above them. The long, haunting wail seemed to carry infinite power. This time, it was a welcome and comforting sound to the little squirrel. It was as if the bird knew all about his pain and was doing something about it.

Fireball's prayers turned into praise, for the Prayer Bird had come!

Meanwhile, the Prayer Bird's continued calling was turning more and more into a wavering, trembling type of laughter, and it was having a terrible effect on the bobcat. It seemed some strange, fiery spirit was entering her ears and burning her from the inside out. She snarled and hissed at the bird, but it would not stop calling! Faster and faster, the bird circled and called, circled and called, circled and called! In futile rage, the cat leaped into the air with claws extended, only to fall on her back in the hot sand. She was losing control of her mind and knew that she had to escape that horrifying sound! So she ran…and ran…and ran across the dunes, all the while with the Prayer Bird following and calling high above her! Fireball could see the vast waters from his lofty lookout and the calls finally ended as the bird  found the horizon above them. The evil bobcat was never seen, or heard from again.

Fireball, on the other hand, returned to living a  semi-normal life of chasing blue jays in the jack pine swale. To this day, blazing fast, smack-talking red squirrels, with their twitching red tails, still look forward to hearing the softly repeated "quick-in-the-needles, quick-in-the-needles" at the start of each summer morning in the Old North Woods.

I cry out to God Most High,
to God who will fulfill his purpose for me.
He will send help from heaven to save me,
rescuing me from those who are out to get me.
My God will send forth his unfailing love
and faithfulness.
Psalm 57: 2-3

Chapter 11

The Thinking Log

Way back in a time that only the ancient trees remember, a chubby little chipmunk lived in a stand of mature beeches and oaks, in the Old North Woods. His home was in a hole in the ground beneath an old decaying log. Long before the chipmunk's time, the log had been a big beech tree that cast an impressive shadow on the forest floor, and the seeds it dropped sprouted into the trees that now looked down upon it. The little chipmunk loved the security of having the log for a roof, and he loved the homey smell of it when he went down into his hole.

Most of all, he loved climbing to the top of his log every evening, when the shadows grew long, and the

Prayer Bird began her calling out on Beaver Tail Lake. It was then that he sat down and took time to think, to listen, and to say a few prayers of his own. Though unseen, every evening the Great Creator warmed his own spot on that log as well. Sometimes the two would have great conversations, and other times it seemed enough just to be near each other and say nothing at all. It was their favorite time of day, and neither would want it to end, but sleepy eyes and tiny little stretches and yawns would send the chipmunk off to bed... well before the dangers of darkness crept in.

The first sound of a beechnut or acorn plopping on the forest floor was all the alarm it took to waken the furry fellow to the next new day. His dirt-gray back and tail, and brown sides blended well with the forest floor as he hurried about, stuffing his oversized cheeks with nuts. Five black and two cream colored stripes running down his back added to his camouflage, while having a slight 'slimming effect' on his plump figure. While one might think this plumpness would make him a slow and easy target, this was not the case, for he was extremely quick and agile. Being hard to see and equally hard to catch kept him from the claws and talons of those who would make a meal of him. Food gathering out in the open was perilous work, but he was well adapted to it.

As autumn set in, a sense of urgency fell upon the Old North Woods. With winter coming, the serious work of preparing for it began, and no one was more serious about it than the chipmunk. Nuts were gathered and stored in his burrow, and once that was full, he buried the rest under dirt and leaves in other secret locations. His survival depended on having this food, both for the long winter and for when he would first emerge from his hole in the spring. As each day became shorter and shorter, he became more obsessed with getting his work done.

As a result, there was less time for talking with neighbors, enjoying the beautiful colored leaves, savoring the taste of a delicious beechnut, or sipping the cool water at the lake's edge. He barely noticed the world around him. As the other animals began to wrap up their fall chores, they noticed that the chipmunk was still working as hard as ever. 'Certainly he has enough food stored by now,' they thought. Truthfully, several chipmunks could live on the amount of food he had stored, with no problem at all!

The most unfortunate result of the chipmunk's hoarding of food was the time he missed atop his log in the evenings. As the days went by, he learned to ignore the Prayer Bird's call, and he worked later and later after sunset. 'There will be time for sitting later,' he reasoned, 'right now more important things need to be done.' Meanwhile, the Great Creator dearly missed his friend as he sat alone on the log each evening, waiting for him to return.

The voices of the forest change as darkness falls. The sound of the loon becomes coyote howls and  hoots of owls. Our distracted chipmunk friend would have been wise to notice these changes as he worked longer into the night. It was only a matter of time before the inevitable happened...and it did.

One night, as the chipmunk buried one last acorn, far too far from the safety of his hole, something came silently out of the darkness and lifted him from the earth. He felt great pain as a talon dug into the side of his face. As she flew, the giant bird made an effort to reposition her prey for a better grip, and the poor chipmunk could think of nothing better to do than bite... and bite he did! Catching the meaty part of the owl's foot in his teeth was a fortunate thing indeed, for this caused the owl to drop him, and he hit the ground running! Before she had turned back to make a second pass, the little rascal was already in his hole. A long and somewhat angry "Hoo, hoo, hooo-aw!" faded in the distance.

The next morning, no chipmunk came out from the hole under the log. It was not until evening that the wounded chipmunk's head popped out and nervously searched for danger. Sensing that the danger had passed, he slowly climbed to the top of his log and sat down to do some things that he hadn't done for a long time: to think, listen, and pray. To his joy, the Great Creator was already sitting there. Waiting, just for him... as usual. They sat in perfect silence, each once again knowing the heart of the other. And somewhere in all his thinking, the little chipmunk wondered why he had ever forgotten the most important things in life. And with that, the Prayer Bird called.

**"Yes, a person is a fool to store up earthly wealth
and not have a rich relationship with God."
Luke 12:21**

Chapter 12

Prophet of the Sky

Way back in a time that only the ancient trees remember, an amazing event took place in the Old North Woods. An event that started with a single falling leaf, and then took wing to change the whole world.

The morning dawned crisp and clear on Beaver Tail Lake, and a light mist gently tiptoed across the glassy waters, almost as if trying not to wake anyone. The only ripples on the entire lake were those rolling off the pale brown breast of a restless young goose as he snuck away from his sleeping family. His shiny black head, adorned with a handsome white chinstrap, stayed low to the water until he had paddled far enough down the lake's edge to be out of sight. He loved being the first on the water on mornings like this, soaking in the first peaceful stirrings of light and life, basking in the glory of it all.

Up ahead, a belted kingfisher slept on a tree limb that stretched out over the water. Normally, getting close to one of these nervous, stubby little birds is nearly impossible. Careful observation revealed that this one's bushy, bluish-gray crest was flat on her noggin, and her keen eyes were closed, which meant the fun was about to begin! The goose silently drifted beneath her and then paused briefly to savor the moment. His white chinstrap feathers looked an awful lot like a mischievous grin. With all his might he struggled not to laugh as he took a deep, quivering breath, and then…

"HON-N-NK!"

...needless to say, the quiet stillness of the morning was no more! It was quite remarkable that the kingfisher was able to save herself from hitting the water. As she flew away, the rattled bird left behind the longest trail of feathers and irritated jabber that ever settled upon Beaver Tail Lake. The goose, on the other hand, exploded into uncontrolled laughter and brief moments of breath control issues. It was the funniest thing he had ever seen in his short life, and he couldn't wait to tell his brothers and sisters about it.

With the fun over, and the calm of the morning broken, it was time for the prankster to make his way back to his family. But destiny would have no part of that, for during her hasty escape, the kingfisher's wing had clipped a leaf, causing it to let loose of its limb. The movement caught the attention of the goose, and he watched the brightly colored object as it drifted this way and that, all the way down, until it settled softly upon the water in front of him. He turned it over with his beak and marveled at the beautiful red and yellow splashes of color. He had

no doubt that this was the artwork of the Great Creator, and he wondered why the green colored leaf of yesterday was no more. Looking up, he saw more painted leaves among the branches, and even though he didn't know why, this sight made his heart all the more restless.

A sudden puff of cool air came and sent the goose's prized leaf sailing away. It danced across the water as if beckoning the goose to join it, and the chase was on! The leaf stayed just out of reach as it led the mesmerized goose farther and farther down the lake. Eventually the pair found themselves in the back end of a large marsh, where the reeds grew tall, and the water took on a golden brown hue as it flowed from a cedar swamp. There, the leaf got trapped between a pair of sticks that stuck up out of the water. Seizing the opportunity, the goose lunged for the leaf and took it in his beak. Once again, it was his!

Perhaps some sort of wilderness justice was being served, for much like the kingfisher, the goose was about to be startled out of his wits. This, because the sticks that caught the leaf were not sticks at all, but the lanky legs of a sandhill crane! When the giant bird croaked out his equally giant "G-o-o-o-o-d mornin'!" the scared goose almost swallowed his leaf as he jumped and stumbled across the surface of the water. The crane's rolling laughter caused the goose to turn and see who had cost him so many feathers. The tall bird was gaunt and ancient looking. His gray feathers were stained brown by his years in the rusty water. A patch of red, wrinkly, featherless skin looked like an old, worn out cap that he wore a bit forward of his gentle eyes. Everything about the bird seemed harmless and inviting, so the goose paddled towards him for a closer look.

The crane bowed slightly and initiated the conversation again, "G-o-o-o-o-d mornin' young fellow. That's a v-e-r-r-r-r-y nice leaf you have there."

The embarrassed goose had forgotten the leaf was still in his beak, and he placed it under his wing for safekeeping. With the leaf out of the way, he could now speak, "Good morning to you sir, please forgive my rude and clumsy intrusion into your day!"

To which the crane replied, "A-a-a-all is well, my heart is lighter because of it, and besides, I was expecting you."

"Expecting me?" the goose questioned, "How can this be, when I don't know you, and no one told me to come here?"

The crane dipped his head down low and whispered in the goose's ear, "A-a-a-ah, but did not the leaf guide you here? And who made the leaf, painted the leaf, and provided the breath that moved the leaf? Please do not tell me that you don't know, for I can see it in your restless eyes that you do!"

The goose was shocked and speechless, for it seemed as if the crane were reading his mind. He thought, 'Why would the Great Creator lead me to an old, half-dead crane?'

Immediately after that thought, the crane bellowed, "Ha-ha-ha-a-a! You shall soon know the answer to that as well my friend, for you are the next PROPHET OF THE SKY!"

Suddenly, the old bird's eyes seemed ablaze

with a fire that burned from somewhere deep within him, and he began to dance and sing, as if he were young again! With his wings extended above him, he

 leaped and kicked up his feet and splashed about, calling as loud as he could, "Ha-ro-ay-ay! Ha-ro-ay-ay! Ha-ro-ay-ay-ay!" which in a crane's tongue means, "Prophet! Prophet! Prophe-et!" Then, just as abruptly as he started, he stopped. All was quiet, except for the drops of water that dripped from his feathers, back into the lake. After a brief pause, he shook his feathers dry, winked at the puzzled goose, and simply said… "Listen."

At first, the goose heard nothing. Then, a faint sound came from the sky in the north. It grew louder and louder as it got closer. Eventually, the goose heard the same words again, "Ha-ro-ay-ay! Ha-ro-ay-ay! Ha-ro-ay-ay-ay!" Only now, the song came from a vast choir of sandhill cranes that blackened the sky as they flew graceful circles above the lake. Each time they came around, hundreds of birds peeled off and dropped down to find their place in the marsh.

Eventually, all were assembled around their leader and the awestruck goose, who by now was hiding between the same two 'sticks' that had once caught a leaf. This amused the flock greatly and their singing turned into good-natured laughter. This all ended with one loud, echoing "squawk!" and a stern look from their grandfather crane. Once it was quiet again, he smiled down at the cowering goose and said, "No-o-o-o need to fear my friend, it's your turn to call for your family, if you'd like."

With such a great multitude of towering birds staring at him, the little goose could hardly "honk" at all. Still, the desperate and feeble "honk" he made was not only enough to summon his immediate family; once again, the whole sky turned black. This time it was geese, and their numbers rivaled the cranes! Such a wondrous sight and sound it was. The air was full of deep musical honking that sounded like

 "Ka-ronk! Ka-ronk! Ka-ronk!" which of course, in goose

language, also meant "Prophet! Prophet! Prophet!"

The young goose's courage grew as more and more of his kindred cupped their wings and settled on the lake. Caught up in the moment, he wished to give his own thankful tribute to the crane. His elated spirit climbed out of his chest, up his long throat, and escaped triumphantly out of his open bill! Gone was the sad "honk" of a scared and restless bird...

"Ka-ronk! Ka-ronk! Ka-ronk!"

This, in turn, caused the whole host to erupt into a deafening song of celebration, and all the creatures of the Old North Woods gathered 'round the lake to witness the spectacle. It was such a joyous occasion that even the kingfisher came. Forgetting any grudge, and putting on her best smile, she hovered just above the goose and crane on rapidly beating wings. The crest on her noggin was now fully erect, and her eyes carried the same strange flame that the crane possessed. 'How odd,' the goose thought, 'who is this kingfisher?' He began to feel ashamed of how he had treated her, and he tried to call out his regret above the loud singing. Three times he tried, while getting louder with each effort...

"I'm sorry. I'm sorry! I'm so sorry!"

Even so, she seemed unable to hear.

Suddenly, she dropped out of the air as if dead! As she plunged beneath the surface, a huge shockwave of watery rings and spray startled the entire throng into complete silence. Stranger yet, was the sight of the water refusing to return to the place where she had fallen. A small island rose up, and upon

it stood not one, but two birds! One was the amazing little kingfisher, and the other was a magnificent white gull, who happened to be missing a leg.

Immediately, all present felt compelled to bow.

The familiar voice of the Great Creator broke the silence, speaking from the wounded gull, in everyone's language, with a love that touched every heart.

He said, "My friends, welcome to The Day of the Prophet! The long southward migration is about to begin and you must ready yourselves for it. The Elder Crane has faithfully guided you and your families on this journey many, many times. My breath has carried him, and all of you, southward in the autumn, and back again in the spring. As you crossed over the earth, My Spirit gave him the words to lead you in song. He boldly testified on my behalf, as my prophet. Well done, Elder Crane!"

A thunderous and sustained cheer went up amongst the crowd, and the crane bowed humbly before his Creator and King. The goose couldn't imagine why he had behaved so badly in the presence of the one that the Great Creator called 'Elder Crane.' As the cheering subsided, and at the nod of the Great Creator, the crane spoke to the goose:

"Ye-e-e-s, my body has flown on many migrations, but now it is very tired. If I were to leave the Old North Woods on this journey, I would not return. My remaining days are few, and the Great Creator is allowing me to spend them here, in the place that I love most dearly. You are a strong young gander, restless for adventure, and a fine replacement for me! Please do not think you are unfit for the task. For who was it that called your kindred here, in such numbers that they blackened the sky? And who carries the treasured leaf beneath his wing, knowing that it is a masterpiece of the Great Creator? Could it be that the One who raises islands, and moves a small fallen leaf, now chooses to move you?"

The goose timidly looked to the Great Creator as if asking for confirmation to what the crane was saying. The all-knowing gull responded by asking a question of His own, "I seem to be missing a leaf. Do you have it?" The goose quickly fumbled beneath his wing and extracted the beautiful leaf, holding it up for its Creator, and all others to see. The Great Creator laughed a wonderful, long, gull-like laugh and said, "So there it is!" He turned to the kingfisher standing next to Him and asked; "Is this the leaf you knocked out of the tree for me?" His trusted servant smirked and nodded as she deliberately made eye contact with the goose. With that, a hearty chuckle moved through the crowd, as the prankster realized that he had been the victim of his own prank! If a soon-to-be-prophet-goose could blush, he would have!

But the goose's thoughts did not linger on that matter. Other things seemed far more important now. Never could he have dreamed that there would be a day when he would share Beaver Tail Lake with such an impressive company of birds, stand in the presence of a prophet crane and kingfisher, and bow before the

Great Creator Himself! Overwhelmed by it all, he paddled forward, stepped on the island, and placed his leaf on the ground before the Great Creator. Turning to the kingfisher he said, "Thank you so much for the part you played in bringing me into His presence." Then he looked the Elder Crane straight in the eye and promised, "I will try to lead the great flocks as faithfully and bravely as you did." Finally, once again, he bowed low before his Creator and King and said these simple words,

"I'll go! Send me."

The Spirit of the Great Creator entered the goose at that moment, empowering him to tell everyone about Him everywhere. The eyes of the goose were now ablaze with a fire that burned from somewhere deep within, and the Great Creator proclaimed for all to hear,

**"This is my chosen one,
the PROPHET OF THE SKY!
Hear his migration song!"**

Obediently, the Prophet Bird began to sing the message that all migratory birds sing to this very day-

"All creatures of the wing
Are born to call, are born to sing-
To tell the news across the land,
That the lives of all are in His hand!"

The little goose led flocks of thousands upon thousands southward that autumn. All shapes and sizes of birds joined him, but it was the geese and the cranes who were the loudest singers. Creatures from around the world heard their message as they flew overhead, and they fell in love with the One who cared enough to send them.

Please, do not forget this story my friends. Do not think that a bird's sole guide is only some primitive instinct to avoid inclement weather. Listen to their song! Let your spirit rise to it. For the One who made their song, made you as well!

Beaver Tail Lake seemed very empty and quiet after the flocks of birds left that day. A lone loon sat motionless upon the dark waters in the middle of the lake. After a long, last look around her, she too ran across the water and took flight into the graying sky. She called a long, haunting, farewell as she circled high above a very small island...an island where an old crane began dancing and singing in the company of a one-legged gull.

"Farewell, Prayer Bird! Farewell!"

Ask the animals, and they will teach you.
Ask the birds of the sky, and they will tell you.
Speak to the earth, and it will instruct you.
Let the fish of the sea speak to you.
They all know that the LORD has done this.
For the life of every living thing is in his hand...
Job 12:7-10

Made in the USA
Lexington, KY
22 May 2018